Daniel Goodwin

In Memory of Robert C. Winthrop

Daniel Goodwin

In Memory of Robert C. Winthrop

ISBN/EAN: 9783744653268

Printed in Europe, USA, Canada, Australia, Japan

Cover: Foto ©Raphael Reischuk / pixelio.de

More available books at **www.hansebooks.com**

IN MEMORY

OF

ROBERT C. WINTHROP

BY

DANIEL GOODWIN

BEFORE THE CHICAGO LITERARY CLUB, NOVEMBER 26, 1888
AND THE CHICAGO HISTORICAL SOCIETY
NOVEMBER 20, 1894

———— ——

CHICAGO
PRIVATELY PRINTED
1894

The Lakeside Press
R. R. DONNELLEY & SONS CO., CHICAGO

CONTENTS.

INTRODUCTION.

The first thought which occurred to me when I learned of the death of Robert C. Winthrop was the great Eulogist has surrendered, and all the scholars of the English and French speaking nations of the world owe his memory a return in kind.

Webster and Everett, Choate and Phillips were his rivals in popular oratory; Bancroft and Prescott, Ellis and Frothingham, Parkman and Motley were his rivals as historians; Story and Quincy, Holmes and Lowell, vied with him in graceful and courteous table talk and post-prandial eloquence: but I know of no record of any man who has had such opportunities 'and who has so perfectly satisfied the hopes and tender anxieties of relatives and friends in pronouncing fitting eulogies upon the great dead of America. Nor has he been the eulogist of Americans alone. Connected by blood with some of the noblest families in England he has, since 1847, been acquainted with the foremost men of Great Britain and France, and as President of the Massachusetts Historical Society and chief trustee of George Peabody he has told the story of most of the great men who have been gathered among the stars for the last fifty years.

The numerous societies, historical, religious and philanthropic, of which he was a member; the city of his birth and death; the congress of the country where he was once Speaker and Senator will, in due time and with proper ceremony, weave for him those laurel leaves which the Muse of history prepares for the great of earth. In the meantime I present to a few of my own friends the tribute I prepared for Mr. Winthrop in 1888 for the Chicago Literary Club, with the addition of an appendix illustrating possibly the man and his surroundings confident in the hope that they will appreciate them as the humble tribute of one who most highly honored his subject, and was grateful for his friendship.

If any of these pages shall drift from the "world's White City" to our Eastern seaboard, let it be remembered by those who may peruse them, that they are the spontaneous tribute of a western friend who is alone responsible for the choice of subjects considered, for the genealogical chart constructed entirely from material in our own Historical and Newberry Libraries and for the meagre glance at Mr. Winthrop's political career, which has been almost entirely ignored in deference to the warmth of sentiments felt by so many of his contemporaries and their successors.

The following Essay was read before the Chicago Literary Club on the 26th of November, 1888, Mr. James L. High, President; Mr. Henry S. Boutell, Secretary pro tem.

OUR SUPREME EULOGIST.

When Robert C. Winthrop, as president of the Massachusetts Historical Society, had pronounced his eulogy upon the memory of his associate, John Lothrop Motley, he called upon James Russell Lowell to follow him. Mr. Lowell began in language which has met my eye since my present subject was chosen, but which seemed to me very expressive and significant. He said, "Mr. President, you assign me a duty of whose danger you only are unconscious, in asking me to add anything to the words of one who by common consent is a master in the perilous oratory of commemoration."

Perilous and difficult indeed many of us have found it, and it may not be labor lost to occupy the hour assigned to us to-night in a brief study of the life, the works, the character and the style of that man who has been so by common consent, in the chief home of our literature and arts, denominated the master of eulogy.

Who of us has not been led into that perilous walk by some strong chord of sympathy or affection? Certainly no clergyman has ever escaped it, either as a duty or a choice, and rare indeed are the lawyers, or physicians, or artists, or men of business, or soldiers surviving from the tented

field who have not been called upon to record
their admiration or their love for friends who
have fallen before them and whose memories
they were not willing to let die.

From the cradle of the human race—from the
first green sod that covered the stricken and life-
less form of the first man to this hour, the world
has been sounding and reverberating the eulogies
of the dear departed. Poetry and music have
given their perpetual offering; the flowers of the
field and the garden have mutely expressed their
sweet and tender remembrance; the orator and
historian have with sonorous sentence and
eloquent illustration recorded the virtues of the
departed.

Most of these eulogies have passed away like
the flowers over which they were spoken, their
transient loveliness all gone with the occasion for
which they grew; and when we have found a
man whose speech is golden, whose words of
eulogy have been set in the volumes of our permanent literature, and when we find that he has
said the right things, at the fitting time and place,
concerning more than a hundred of the
uncrowned kings of thought, and literature, and
statesmanship, covering more than half of this
most wonderful of all the centuries since the
world began, we may well pause and look a little
into the sources and causes of such marked excel-
lence, such countless endeavor, such perfect success.

I.

HIS FAMILY AND GENEALOGY.

When Thomas Lindall Winthrop married
Elizabeth Bowdoin Temple in Boston, Massachusetts, July, 1786, the wedding brought
together in one ancestral tree a very rare and
remarkable union of families; the most rare and
most remarkable I have ever yet examined.

If you will take the family branches and construct them in the ordinary genealogical style into
a great tree, the trunk of which shall be, if you
please, the great orator who forms the topic of
my essay, and call that trunk by the name of
"Robert C. Winthrop," and from it build up the
branches with the names of Winthrops, Temples,
Bowdoins, Ervings, Lyndes, Portages, Lindalls,
Dudleys, Tyngs and Nelsons, you will sound the
names of men and families marked for conspicuous ability and public services for the last three
centuries.

Enumerating his American ancestry alone,
our subject is descended from two Governors
Winthrop; from Chief Justice Wait Winthrop;
from both Governors Thomas and Joseph
Dudley; from Governor James Bowdoin, of
Huguenot blood; from Hon. John Erving, one of
the King's Council before the Revolution; from
Hon. Edward Tyng, one of the King's Council
in 1687; from Hon. Simon Lynde, the father and
grandfather of two Chief Justices Benjamin
Lynde; from Francis Browne, the ancestor also ·

of Justice Joseph Story. His mother's father
was Sir John Temple, the friend of Franklin,
and son-in-law of Gov. Bowdoin. Temple was a
kinsman and protégé of the great Chatham and
the younger Pitt, and of the same family with
Earl Temple and George Grenville, the late
Lord Palmerston and the Dukes of Buckingham
and Chandos, a family distinguished in English
history for nineteen generations.

These distinguished ancestors have also
brought him into collateral kinship with numberless families of deserved prominence, such as the
descendants of Alexander Hamilton, Governor
Stuyvesant, Governor Sullivan, the Amorys and
Sears, Livingstons, Schuylers and Van Rensse-
laers.

II.

HARVARD UNIVERSITY.

To you, gentlemen, who graduated from our
oldest University, the name and fame of Mr.
Winthrop has a peculiar interest.

Harvard University was to him as much an
inheritance as Boston Common, or the old State
House, or Faneuil Hall.

Indeed the University itself was largely
indebted for its very existence to John Winthrop,
who had graduated at Trinity College, Cambridge, England. President Edward Everett, at
the Harvard Second Centennial in 1836, repre-
sented Governor Winthrop as making the speech
which led the legislature of the infant colony to

vote the original endowment under which the college was established, and President Quincy in his history of the university says, " Next to John Harvard, John Winthrop, the leader of the Massachusetts Colony and twelve times its elected governor, deserves grateful commemoration. His donation of books was large and valuable. His name and influence were always given in its support. There is probably no one to whose patronage the college was more indebted during the period of its infancy, weakness and dependence."

Nearly all of his male lineal ancestors had graduated at Harvard for generations, not to mention numberless collaterals. His father was of the class of 1780.

One of his father's grandfathers, Francis Borland, was of the class of 1774, and another of his grandfathers, Governor James Bowdoin, was of the class of 1745, and among his other lineal ancestors were Timothy Lindall of 1695, Governor Thomas Dudley of 1651, and Governor Joseph Dudley of 1665, and John Tyng of 1691.

When Mr. Winthrop entered Harvard, in 1823, we were fairly started on the up-grade of letters and learning, following our second war of independence which terminated so gloriously in 1815, and among his college-mates were numbers who have contributed to the peerless position occupied by our country to-day.

Graduating at nineteen years of age, the third in a class of fifty-three, and with a commencement oration which was soon put into the school-books as a model of English eloquence, he showed from the very start that his family wealth and distinction were not crutches to be leaned on, but that he had inherited the glorious aspiration to toil and labor for the good and glory of mankind.

Some of his speeches at the alumni meetings have been reported and published, and are replete with interesting reminiscences of the great men who had been connected with the university as officers or students in his day.

At the alumni meeting in 1852, he said : " We are here to bless the place of our earliest and best opportunities. We come one and all to bear our united testimony to the value of this venerated institution. We come to bring whatever laurels we have acquired, whatever treasures we have accumulated to adorn its hallowed shrines. We come to pay fresh homage to the memory of our fathers for having founded and reared it. We come to renew our tribute of gratitude to its earlier and its later benefactors. We come to thank God for having prospered and blessed it. And we come, above all, to acknowledge our own personal indebtedness to it and to make public recognition of the manifold obligations and responsibilities to God and man which rest upon us all by reason of the opportunities and advantages which we have here enjoyed.

" We arrogate nothing to ourselves in the way of distinction or privilege. We are not blind to the fact that there are those around us, who have enjoyed none of our academic opportunities, who have outstripped not a few of us, in the practical pursuits of literature and of life. We do not for-

get that there are some of them who have sur-
passed us all in the highest walks of art, of
science, and of patriotic statesmanship.   Honor,
honor this day from this assembled multitude of
scholars to the self-made, self-educated men who
have adorned our country's history. Honor to the
common schools of our land, from which such
men have derived all which they have not owed
to their own industry, their own energy, their own
God-given genius.

"Bowditch, Fulton, Franklin, Washington ;
when will any American university be able to point
to names upon its catalogue of alumni which may
be likened to these names for the originality and
profoundness of the researches, for the practical
importance of the accomplishments, for the gran-
deur and sublimity of the inventions and discov-
eries, or for the noble achievements and glorious
institutions with which they are indissolubly associated?   Well may we say, as we proudly inscribe
their names upon our honorary rolls, 'They were
wanting to our glory, we were not wanting to
theirs.'

"Nor are we here to indulge in any invidious
comparisons between our own Harvard and other
universities and colleges in the state or in the nation.
It is pardonable to love our own mother better
than other people's mothers.   It is natural that
we should

> 'Be to her faults a little blind,
> Be to her virtues very kind.'

"Indeed, as we run our eye over her long list

of children and see what a glorious company she has sent forth into every field of Christian service, and follow her along her starry way for more than two centuries, we might be almost pardoned for forgetting that she has or ever had any faults. Could we but see something of a higher moral discipline, something of a deeper religious sentiment, something of a stronger spiritual influence mingling with the sound scholarship which pervades her halls and giving something of a fresher and fuller significance to her ancient motto, ' *Christo et Ecclesiae*,' there would be little or nothing more to be desired in her condition."

I have quoted but the prelude to his oration on the obligations and responsibilities of educated men. One other page of it seems to me to so fully show forth the vital principle and the style of the man that I cannot forbear quoting it :

" How much better, and purer, and nobler a literature might we not have, and how much more just and elevated a public sentiment as its result, if every man who is educated to the use of the pen or of the tongue could be made to feel within himself, as he sits down to his desk or rises to the rostrum, 'The word that I write or that I speak to-day is not for the moment or for myself alone. It is not mine to minister merely to my own pleasure, to my own profit, to my own fame. It is not mine to pander to some popular delusion, to fan some popular prejudice, to flatter some popular favorite, or to adorn some plausible falsehood. It is to produce an influence far beyond that which it immediately proposes. It is to enter,

somewhere, in a greater or less degree, into the
very springs and issues of human action. It may
influence individuals. It may influence masses.
It cannot rest indifferent. It cannot return unto
me empty. It will mingle with the great current
of public opinion in some part of its course where
it winds through some quiet valley, or takes its
way beneath some cottage window, if not where
it foams and roars around some splendid capital or
some mighty metropolis. This very word which
I speak or write to-day may rouse up a resolute
human soul to a newer and better life, or it may
turn back some timid and wavering spirit from its
truest and best ends, unsettle its faith, unship its
anchor, and leave it wrecked for time and for eter-
nity. It may stir the breast of a mighty nation to
the maintenance of law or the vindication of liberty; or it may stimulate and infuriate it to the
overthrow of the noblest institutions, in a mad pur-
suit of impracticable philanthropies and reforms.
It may elevate and ennoble the hopes, and views,
and aims of mankind, and advance the cause of
peace on earth and good-will among men; or it
may blow up the smouldering embers of interna-
tional strife, and kindle a conflagration which
shall wrap a world in flames. I am, I must be,
responsible for the result."

Those of you who have had the privilege of
visiting the Memorial Hall and Sanders' Theatre
in Cambridge, may feel interested in recognizing
Mr. Winthrop's aid in starting those beautiful
buildings. On the 17th July, 1857, (Vol.
II, 354.) he presided at the Alumni meet-

2

ing, and after eloquently praising the host of laborers who were there trained up and sent forth into every field and vineyard of church and of state, of theology, medicine, law, literature, science, philosophy, commerce, legislation, philanthropy and patriotism, he expressed a longing for some ample and commodious hall for the secular services and festivals of the university.

He said, " I envy the individual name which shall be inscribed on such a building. I have sometimes ventured to cherish the hope that the Alumni as an Association might be willing and able to undertake the work, and that a stately and commodious hall like the Senate house at Old Cambridge or the Theatre at Oxford might be seen standing on some appropriate spot of the college grounds bearing on its front, 'The Alumni of Harvard to their '*Alma Mater*,"' where the exhibitions, and Class days, and Commencements of the University might find worthy accommodations ; where the living alumni might hold their anniversary festivals and where the memorials of the distinguished dead might find a fit gallery for their display."

Within forty-eight hours after Mr. Winthrop's speech was reported, Mr. Charles Sanders, of the class of 1802, started the scheme to which he ultimately gave more than $60,000 and by his efforts greatly aided in procuring that remarkable building.

III.

MR. WINTHROP, THE STATESMAN.

Coming upon the historic stage with the widest range of distinguished ancestors, our subject was fortunate in the time and place of his advent. He was born in Boston, on the 12th of May, 1809, in the house occupied by his father, Lieutenant-Governor Winthrop, and belonging to James Bowdoin, minister to Spain and patron of Bowdoin College. He attended the Latin school on School Street where the Parker House now stands (which was kept by Samuel Greeley the father of our genial brother Samuel S. Greeley), and he here won the Franklin medal and a gold medal for a Latin poem.

After graduating at Harvard in 1828 he studied law under Daniel Webster, and was admitted to the bar in 1831. On the 23d of October, 1833, when twenty-four years old, on behalf of the young men of Boston, he made the welcoming speech to Henry Clay at the Tremont, and indicated the cardinal principles which revealed the needle of that political compass by which he, and almost he alone, has been guided for more than half a century. Few indeed of his contemporaries or his successors but have been led by some influence, or forced by some circumstances, to change their course or their principles, but a close examination of the record of Mr. Winthrop from 1833 to 1888 will show the same old conservative Whig, devoted to the Constitution and the Union, opposed to slavery wherever the Constitution permitted opposition, opposed everywhere to its extension, and in favor of universal education, proper protection to our trade and manufactures, and the largest possible development of internal improvements.

In 1834 he was elected to the Massachusetts house, and in 1835 he made a speeeh remarkable for its eloquence, its fire, its lofty spirit of liberality and justice in favor of compensating the Catholics for the destruction of the Ursuline convent in Charleston by a mob. (Vol. I, p 174.) He was at this time and for many years an earnest supporter of the Boston militia companies, which by their close connection with the voters are the bulwarks of civil liberty and order. He was captain of the Boston Light Infantry, lieutenant of the Ancient and Honorable Artillery Company, and on the staff of three successive Governors, John Davis, Samuel T. Armstrong and Edward Everett.

In December, 1838, he delivered an address before the Boston Lyceum on Free Schools and Free Governments, taking advanced ground upon the importance of political education, holding "that children should be educated as those by whom the destinies of the Nation are one day to be wielded, and free schools cherished as places in which those destinies are even now to be woven." He has inculcated the same principles for fifty years, and he, more than any man, stamped them upon the great mind of General Grant, whom he had brought into the board of trustees of the Peabody fund, and had the pleasure of reading that

great hero's declaration at the army reunion in
1875, in Iowa, when General Grant said, " Let us
labor for the security of free thought, free speech,
free press, pure morals, unfettered religious sentiment, and equal rights and privileges for all men,
irrespective of nationality, color or religion; en-
courage free schools, and resolve that neither State
nor Nation shall support any institution save those
where every child may get a common-school education unmixed with any atheistic, pagan, or sectarian teaching."

In 1839 Mr. Winthrop's reputation outgrew
its local celebrity at Boston, and he delivered an
address at New York City in December on the
" Pilgrim Fathers," which gave evidence of his
full appreciation of the wonderful work done by
his forefathers and that the eternal fitness of
things demanded great, permanent and national
work from himself. He had been a member of
the Massachusetts house for five years, and had
the honor of being elected its Speaker at an
earlier age than any one before or since. He had
been married and given hostages to fortune in the
shape of two sons, who still survive—a solace to
his old age.

In 1840 the name and fame of Mr. Winthrop
became the property of the nation. With the
ardor of a youth of thirty-one and the concen-
trated energies of as good Puritan and Huguenot
blood as ever flowed, with the eloquence of a
Massachusetts patriot and the well-balanced judg-
ment of a disciple of Washington and Franklin,
he went into the campaign of 1840 with General

Harrison and was triumphantly elected to Congress as sole Representative from Boston.

In this connection it may be well to state Mr. Winthrop's understanding of the creed of the Whig party, because they have been the principles upon which he has acted all his life.

In his interesting and instructive eulogy upon Henry Clay, in August, 1879, after he entered upon his seventy-first year, Mr. Winthrop said:

"What was this Whig party which he led so gallantly, before disappointed ambition, and inconsiderate philanthropy, and headlong fanaticism and secret know-nothing lodges, and corrupt coalitions at one end of the Union conspired with mad and monstrous schemes in the interest of African slavery at the other end to draw off so many of its members into new ranks, and doom it to a lingering death? What was the party of which Henry Clay and Daniel Webster were so long the shining lights, and of which Abraham Lincoln was so long one of the luminaries?

"It was a constitutional union party, which regarded the union of the States and the Federal Constitution as the only formal condition and bond of that Union, as things to be reverenced and maintained at all hazards. It was a law and order party, which tolerated no revolutionary or riotous processes of reform. It was a party of principle and purity, which consented to no corruption or traffic as a means of securing office or success. It was a conservative party, and yet a party of progress which looked to the elevation of American labor and the advancement of our

national welfare by a discriminating adjustment
and an equitable collection of duties on imports,
by an honest currency, by a liberal administration
of the public lands, and by needful appropriations
from time to time for the improvement of rivers
and harbors.   It was a party of peace—domestic
peace and foreign peace—opposed to every law-
less scheme of encroachment or aggrandizement,
at home or abroad, and studiously avoiding whatever might occasion internal commotion or
external conflict.   It was above all things a
national party, extending over the whole .
country and systematically renouncing and repu-
diating all merely sectional organizations or
issues."

Will it not somewhat puzzle the students of our
next century to understand how it was that a
small body of Free-soilers combining with the
Conservative Democracy of Massachusetts could
be able to defeat such a man as Winthrop, so true
to the principles prevailing in his state?   When
they had elected Mr. Sumner his successor, he was
forced to plant himself practically upon the platform of Mr. Winthrop.   He said (works of
Sumner, Vol. 2, p. 429) :

"We propose to wait and work patiently under
and through the Constitution that our purposes
may be peaceably accomplished in the spirit of
that instrument and of our fathers.   We are con-
stitutionalists and Unionists.   We reverence the
Constitution of the United States and seek to
guard it against infractions, believing that under
the Constitution Freedom can be best preserved.

We reverence the union of the States, believing
that the peace, happiness and welfare of all de-
pend upon this blessed bond."

Nay, the Republican party itself was obliged to
stand upon Mr. Winthrop's platform, and after
Mr. Lincoln was elected President, solemn resolutions were adopted by us, in and out of Congress, pledging our party not to interfere with
slavery in the states and offering to embody it by
an amendment to the constitution itself.

Mr. Winthrop was constantly reëlected from
Boston for ten years, and in 1850 was appointed
United States Senator to fill the position vacated
by Daniel Webster, who went into President
Fillmore's Cabinet. These were ten years of
active service. His youth and energy, his happy
command of illustration, both from books and
life, his genial and persuasive address, his splendid
social position, and his intimate acquaintance with
the leading scholars and statesmen of Great
Britain and France made him the favorite leader
of the House under Henry Clay and Daniel
Webster, and lifted him in 1847, when only
thirty-eight years old, to the Speakership of the
House, a position regarded by many as the most
honorable, as well as one of the most influential,
under our Government. It is possible for an
inferior man to be elected President or Vice-President, but not as Speaker of the House, which
chooses its own presiding officer.

Mr. Winthrop's career as Speaker was
eminently successful. The late Mr. Charles E.
Hazewell said, "It was a common remark, and no

one heard it without assenting to the truth of the
words expressed, 'Mr. Winthrop was born for
the chair.'" Mr. James G. Blaine says, "The
chief reason for his selection as Speaker was his
preëminent fitness for the important post.   He
was but thirty-eight years of age, but he earned
so valuable a reputation as a presiding officer that
some of his decisions have been quoted as pre-
cedents in the National House and have been
incorporated in permanent works on ' Parliamen-
tary Law.'"

In 1841 he made an elaborate speech on the
tariff, in favor of protection to American labor
and manufactures (Vol. 2, p. 306.) In 1843 he
submitted, in behalf of the Committee on Commerce, strong resolutions against the imprison-
ment of free colored seamen from vessels touching at ports in the Southern States.

In 1844, when the great question as to the right
of petition came before the House, and whether the
anti-slavery petitions from Massachusetts presented by John Q. Adams should be received,
Mr. Winthrop made a powerful speech in their
support, breathing the liberty-laden air of
Faneuil Hall and the Old South Church.   He
argued for "the inherent and inextinguishable
elasticity of opinion, of conscience, of inquiry,
which, like the great agent of modern art, gains
only new force, fresh vigor, redoubled powers of
progress and propulsion by every degree of com-
pression and restraint; it is this to which the
world owes all the liberty it has yet acquired, and
to which it will owe all that is yet in store for it.

Well did John Milton exclaim in his noble defense of unlicensed printing, 'Give me liberty to know, to utter, and to argue freely above all liberties,' for in securing that we secure the all-sufficient instrument for achieving all other liberties."

In January, 1845, Mr. Winthrop made a powerful speech against the annexation of Texas upon the ground that it involved an extension of domestic slavery, and he made several speeches against the war with Mexico as an unjust contest for the acquisition of territory.

While recognizing the constitutional rights of the South to some provision for the return of fugitives, he refused to consent to any law which did not provide for a fair trial by jury and the writ of *habeas corpus.*

He said, " I hold it to be a just and reasonable provision, and one which ought to form a part of any bill which shall be passed for this purpose. There is a preliminary question, and that is whether he is a fugitive at all, whether he belongs or owes service to anybody. It must always be a question whether such a person be your slave or whether he be our freeman — a question which should be tried where he is seized and when the immediate liberty which he enjoys is about to be taken away from him. I am in favor of recognizing the right of trial by jury in all cases where a question of personal liberty is concerned."

It was while Mr. Winthrop was Speaker of the House, in 1848, that the great opportunity of his lifetime occurred in being selected to pronounce the oration when the corner-stone of the Washington monument was laid.

When the corner-stone of Bunker Hill monument was laid, in 1825, there was anxious and careful consultation as to who should pronounce the oration. The choice fortunately fell upon Daniel Webster, whose oration, as Mr. Winthrop said, "shook the school-benches of New England," and passed into the classics of a language which the genius of Webster has shown to be the strongest, the subtlest, the smoothest, the best of modern times. When that magnificent monument was completed, in 1843, there was no anxiety, no discussion, no doubt as to what orator should stand beside it, for all the world felt that no voice but Webster's should announce the words "It is finished." And so it was with the still grander monument to Washington in our national capital. When its corner-stone was laid, in 1848, it was a matter of thought, discussion and anxiety as to who should give expression to a nation's reverence for its greatest and most representative character and hero. The choice fell almost by accident upon a young man less than forty years of age. Most eloquently did the young orator perform his difficult task, and when after thirty-seven years of labor and trial these United States had through the convulsions of civil war become fused into a compact and solidified Nation, and finished the grandest monument ever erected by a Nation to the honor of a single man, there was among our fifty millions of peo-

ple no doubt or discussion as to who should pronounce the words "It is finished." Without
distinction of party or locality, of creed or color,
both North and South, East and West, moved by
a common impulse pronounced the name of Robert C. Winthrop, of Massachusetts.

Mr. Winthrop's seventeen years of political
service came to an end in 1851. A coalition
between the most radical wing of Free-soilers and
the pro-slavery Democracy divided the offices and
defeated the conservative, anti-slavery Whig party.

After a hard fought battle the coalitionists
triumphed carrying both branches of the Legislature, but the conflict for Senator went on for
months, and Charles Sumner was at last chosen
by a bare majority. On the 26th ballot April 24,
1851, 384 votes were cast, 193 being necessary to
a choice. Mr. Winthrop received the full Whig
vote 166, Mr. Henry W. Bishop, (the father of
our brother member) received 11, and Mr. Sumner 193 votes, mostly Democrats and a few Free-
soilers. At the next State Election the Whigs
insisted on running Mr. Winthrop for Governor.
He received 60,000 votes, the Democrats cast 40,000
for George S. Boutwell, and the Free-soilers
30,000 for the eminent historian John G. Palfrey.
The constitution at that time required a majority
of all votes and so the election was thrown into
the House, and the coalition elected Governor
Boutwell.

Since 1852 Mr. Winthrop refused all political
candidacies and appointments, and has devoted
himself to literature, to history, to philanthropy.

IV.

PRESIDENT OF THE MASSACHUSETTS HISTORICAL SOCIETY.

Mr. Winthrop was a member of the Massachusetts Historical Society for nearly sixty years, and was its president for thirty years, from 1855 to 1885. It is the oldest and leading society of its kind in America, and composed of such men as the Adamses, Quincys, Everetts, Motley, Prescott, Saltonstall, Samuel Hoar and his sons, the Judge and Senator; Palfrey, Bancroft, Ellis, Parkman, and Winsor.

V.

ARTS AND SCIENCES.

He was also for forty years an active member of the American Academy of Arts and Sciences; established in 1780, in the midst of our Revolutionary War, by his great grandfather, Governor Bowdoin, who was its first president. Among its other presidents were the three illustrious Adamses—John Adams, John Quincy Adams and Charles Francis Adams. Among its members were Franklin, Faraday, Rumford, Agassiz, Audubon, Arago, Bache, Sir David Brewster, Darwin, Humboldt, Lafayette and the Lowells.

It is difficult to overestimate the past and possible future benefit of this society to the world. At its centennial, in 1880, Mr. Winthrop remarked:

"Could the founders of this academy even now look down from the skies upon our own little State of Massachusetts, with what rapture would they behold encircling this academy as their original nucleus a natural history society, with its manifold and growing collections and cabinets; a technological institute, with its admirable curriculum of scientific education; a splendid museum of the fine arts; an observatory, with its comet-seekers and transit instruments, and with its noble refractor; the Lawrence Scientific School; the chemical laboratory of Prof. Cooke; the garden and herbarium of our great botanist, Dr. Gray; the magnificent Agassiz Museum of Comparative Zoölogy, and close at its side the Peabody Museum of Archæology and Ethnology; and all our thriving associations of history and literature and music, of horticulture and agriculture; and, better than all, the hosts of busy and devoted students in these and other institutions, who are engaged day by day and night by night in searching out the mysteries of nature, and extorting from her so many of the secrets which have been hid from all human eyes and all human conceptions from the foundations of the world!

"They would be heard exclaiming with one accord, in the sublime words with which our first president concluded his inaugural discourse a hundred years ago, 'Great and marvelous are Thy works, Lord God Almighty; in wisdom hast Thou made them all!'"

VI.

Mr. Winthrop was president of the Boston Provident Association for twenty-five years, working with such men as Dr. Peabody, Dr. Lothrop, Bishop Huntington and others. When he retired, in 1879, the Executive Committee said of him, "He brought to us not only the respect due to eminent national services and an honored name, but the power of organization and skill in administration which were natural to his character and had been matured by experience of weighty and conspicuous public affairs. His constant and punctual presence at our meetings has added both dispatch and dignity to the transaction of our business. His name has brought to us the most important of the legacies which we have received, and it is within bounds to say that for the generous endowment of our association we are as much indebted to him as if it had been his direct gift. The future historian of Boston can never pass by the important services which Mr. Winthrop has rendered to its charities."

Mr. Winthrop was a member of the vestry of Trinity Church, Boston, for nearly sixty consecutive years, and a delegate to the General Convention of the Protestant Episcopal church in America for more than a quarter of a century. His record, however, as a Christian was too broad to be hemmed in even by that most beautiful of all the parish churches in Christendom. He had the good fortune to worship for nearly thirty years with his grand Christian rector, Phillips Brooks,

who was born in Boston at about the period when
Mr. Winthrop was first elected a vestryman of
old Trinity.   Mr. Winthrop was president of the
Massachusetts Bible Society and connected with
many other religious societies.   Not the least interesting of his addresses are those to the Bible
societies and Young Men's Christian Associations.
I would call attention especially to that one delivered April 9, 1859, at Boston, and repeated on
May 5, 1859, at Richmond, Va., on " Christianity,
neither Sectarian nor Sectional, the Great Remedy
for Social and Political Evils," from which we
take the following extracts (Vol. II, pp. 418 et
seq.)

" Few persons can contemplate the present im-
proved condition of the Christian world without
lamenting that the best energies of Christian
sects are still so often employed in criticising, cen-
suring and condemning each other.   I pray
heaven that no accident and still more that no de-
sign may revive the slumbering embers of religious strife.   Rarely does the strongest side prevail
or even come off best from such encounters.   Not
often does even the right side, whether it be
strongest or weakest, escape from them without
damage or detriment.   Principles indeed can
never be conceded nor compromised.   We can
never abandon the Bible, even in the schools.
We can never compromise the Lord's prayer or
the ten commandments.   We cannot spare a note
or a chord of the time-honored and glorious har-
monies of Old Hundred.   Yet everything except
principles, everything that is merely formal and

conventional, may well be the subject of concilia-
tory arrangement under proper circumstances, and
at the proper time for the sake of Christian peace.
I can never think of the bitterness and rancor
which is so often allowed to enter into religious
differences and controversies, without remember-
ing how much our religious opinions, our religious
creeds, our religious connections have been determined—pre-determined, providentially determined
—for us all by the mere influence of early and
seemingly accidental associations.   The place of
our birth, the circumstances of our condition, the
surroundings of our childhood, the fascination of
some beloved and faithful pastor the paternal pre-
cept and example, the mother's knee, the family
pew have after all done more to decide for each
one of us the peculiarities of our religious faith
and of our religious forms than all the catechisms
of assemblies, the decrees of councils or the canons
of convocations.   We delight to worship God
where our fathers and mothers worshipped him,
to kneel at the same altar at which they knelt, to
unite in the same prayers or it may be to utter the
same responses, in which their voices were once
heard and which they first taught us to lisp or to
listen too as children.   The memories of fathers   √
and mothers and brothers and sisters with whom
we have "taken sweet counsel together and
walked to the house of God in company" cluster
sweetly around us as we sit in the old seats and
sing the old psalms and hymns.   We almost
shrink from trying to get to heaven by any other
road than that which they traveled, lest we should

miss them at our journey's end. Every man
who has opportunity and education should read
the gospel of Christ for himself and bring the
best lights within his reach to aid him in its inter-
pretation. But mysteries there are in that gospel
which constrained even the great apostle to say,
"Here we see through a glass, darkly." Mysteries there are which the reason of the natural
man was never made or intended to penetrate;
which it may be were expressly designed to
humble the presumption and confound the pride
and mortify the vanity of mere human wisdom,
and to leave larger room for the childlike graces
of humility and faith, and the speculative differences which such mysteries must ever and inevita-
bly engender should be regarded with mutual
deference and charity—never forgetting that it
were an impeachment of the love of God and an
imputation upon the mercy of Christ, to imagine
that the essential elements of a true Christian faith
have been placed beyond the easy reach and ready
acceptance even of the humblest and simplest understanding." II. 422.

"I hail this union of young men of so many different Christian sects in a single association for
Christian ends and objects, as a pledge that the
jealousies and rivalries which have so long divided
the church of Christ on earth, will be more as-
suaged and extinguished, that religious men of all
denominations will more and more bear in mind
the great and glorious things in which they all
agree, and will strive to narrow instead of wid-
ening their causes of alienation and estrangement.

The day may come when the cause of Christianity may require the cordial and vigorous union of all who acknowledge God as their Father and Christ as their Redeemer and Saviour, and the Bible as the word of God and the only text-book of eternal truth, in order to withstand and resist the progress of a downright infidelity—cloaking itself under a thousand specious forms of positive and speculative philosophy, of materialism, spiritualism and pantheism. Let us prepare seasonably for such a day, and for the conflicts it will involve by uniting together in a league of Christian charity—holding our faith in the unity of the Spirit and in the bond of peace. Let us pursue our Christian work in the true spirit of Christianity —a spirit of love to God and of love to man— maintaining our peculiar and distinctive tenets firmly but never arrogantly, boldly but never offensively, uncompromisingly but never aggressively ; ever respecting our neighbor's conscience as we claim our neighbor's respect for our own conscience, and not forgetting that our final responsibilities are not to each other but to that common Master before whom we must stand or fall. Who does not rejoice, as Sunday after Sunday comes round, to see the multitudes that keep holy day, thronging our streets and sidewalks and exchanging the smiles of recognition or the greetings of friendship or the formalities of ceremony as they make way for each other in passing along to their various places of religious worship. To human eyes indeed they seem to be moving in widely different directions, and so it may prove to have been with some of them; but so have I seen on a summer sea, in yonder bay, alike in calm and in storm, vessels of every sort and beneath every sign, sailing in widely different and diverging courses, crossing and recrossing each other's tracks and seemingly propelled by the most opposite and contrarious forces. Yet the same wind of heaven, blowing where it listeth, was the common source of their motive power, giving impulse and direction to the progress of them all alike, and bringing them all to be moored at last in one common haven of rest."

The broad-minded, beautiful tolerance of Mr. Winthrop is admirably illustrated by the following quotation from his oration on the 250th anniversary of the Landing of the Pilgrims : (Vol. III, p. 105.)

"Let those who will, indulge in the dream, or cherish the waking vision of a single universal church on earth, recognized and accepted of men, whose authority is binding on every conscience and decisive of every point of faith or form. To the eye of God, indeed, such a church may be visible even now in 'the blessed company of all faithful people,' in whatever region they may dwell, with whatever organization they may be connected, with Him as their head 'of whom the whole family in earth and heaven is named.' And as in some grand orchestra, hundreds of performers, each with his own instrument and his own separate score, strike widely variant notes, and produce sounds, sometimes in close succession and sometimes at lengthened intervals, which heard

alone would seem to be wanting in everything
like method or melody, but which heard together
are found delighting the ear and ravishing the
soul with a flood of magnificent harmony, as they
give concerted expression to the glowing conceptions of some mighty master, even so—even so,
it may be,—from the differing, broken, and often
seemingly discordant strains of sincere seekers
after God, the divine ear, upon which no lisp of
the voice or breathing of the heart is ever lost,
catches only a combined and glorious anthem of
prayer and praise.   But to human ears such har-
monies are not vouchsafed. The Church in all its
majestic unity shall be revealed hereafter. The
'Jerusalem which is the mother of us all, is above,'
and we can only humbly hope that in the provi-
dence of God, its gates shall be wider, and its
courts fuller, and its members quickened and mul-
tiplied by the very differences of form and of doc-
trine which have divided Christians from each
other on earth, and which have created something
of competition and rivalry, and even of conten-
tion, in their efforts to advance the ends of their
respective denominations."

VII.

THE PEABODY TRUST.

Great and striking as have been Mr. Winthrop's contributions to politics, to Harvard University, to the charities of his vicinage, to historical and literary work, to the arts and sciences, and

to his beloved church, it seems to me his last work in life, begun at an age when most of us are willing to rest upon our oars and float upon the stream, especially if the current of our lives runs through peaceful and beautiful shores, is the most touching and affecting of all his work.

On the 7th of February, 1867, his friend George Peabody, a philanthropist without precedent or parallel, preëminent among the benefactors of his age and race, like Washington among patriots and Shakespeare among poets, committed to Mr. Winthrop in sacred trust millions of dollars for the intellectual, moral or industrial education of the young of the South, " without other distinction than their needs and the opportunities of usefulness to them." In the first paragraph of Mr. Peabody's letter he alludes to Mr. Winthrop as " the distinguished and valued friend to whom I am so much indebted for cordial sympathy, careful consideration and wise counsel; and the details and organization of the trust I leave with you, only requesting that Mr. Winthrop may be chairman and Governor Fish and Bishop McIlvaine vice-chairmen of your body."

How singular and grand it was that this greatest benefaction of modern times should come from a son of Massachusetts to the poor children of many who had slain thousands of her loveliest sons in battle, and that the descendant of John Winthrop the Puritan should be the chief executor and trustee to those desolate children of the South.

From February, 1867, to the present time the

choicest labor of Mr. Winthrop has been in the execution of this noble trust, and in its execution he has had the hearty coöperation of such men as Bishops McIlvaine and Whipple, Chief Justices Waite and Fuller, Hamilton Fish, General Grant, President Hayes, William M. Evarts, and others of similar eminence.

I will not enter into any detail of the immense amount of work accomplished by this board, but those of you who are teachers can imagine the study and travel and anxiety and responsibility involved when I state that the board has already distributed nearly three millions of money from the income of their fund. They have given to Alabama $89,800; to Arkansas $97,050; to Florida $61,375; to Georgia $102,552; to Louisiana $95,600; to Mississippi $71,378; to North Carolina $131,365; to South Carolina $74,425; to Tennessee $202,700; to Texas $99,850; to Virginia $259,550; to West Virginia $139,000 and to the Normal College at Nashville $303,000.

It is pleasant to be able to state in this connection that the generosity of Mr. Peabody and his Trustees has drawn with its magnet of sympathy other helps in the shape of a donation of 100,000 books from D. Appleton & Co., and about 100,000 more from A. S. Barnes & Co.

No wonder that the name of Winthrop is honored and reverenced all over the lately desolated South, next to that of Washington and Peabody; that States and cities and individuals should have covered his name with blessings. In South Carolina the General Assembly incorporated its training school for teachers by the name of " The Winthrop Training School," and its board "Resolved that the 12th day of May, the birthday of the Hon. Robert C. Winthrop, be set apart as an annual memorial day, in commemoration of the beneficence by which the school was founded."

In this epitome of the records, which could well be amplified into volumes, I have merely sought to explain why it was that Robert C. Winthrop has been so situated, so connected and so gifted as to make him our *"supreme Eulogist."* I know no other man who has had such opportunities, and who has so perfectly realized the hopes and relieved the anxieties of relatives and friends by pronouncing fitting eulogies upon the great dead of his century.

He has survived almost every one of the toilers who kept step with his early years. My hour would not permit me to enumerate even the subjects of his formal eulogies.

Had I a magician's wand which could summon from their homes the spirits of those whose memories have been commemorated by the tongue of Mr. Winthrop, I should draw around us to-night such a company as the world could hardly have duplicated. He has delivered more than one hundred and forty public eulogies, of greater or less length and fullness. Leaving out his peerless Washington the majestic father of his country, and Franklin the great Bostonian, and Governor Bowdoin, and Governor Winthrop,

and Luther and Dante, and a few others whom
he knew only in the spirit and by their words and
works, and confining ourselves only to those
whose hearts were clasped with hooks of living
steel to his own, what a company should we see!

At the head of the column come their country's defenders, those who bared their breasts to
the shot and shell of foreign or domestic enemies
that America, the hope of the world, might be
preserved. Prescott, Knox, Lafayette, Rocham-
beau, Steuben, Dearborn, Preble, Sullivan,
Decatur, Scott, Harrison, Taylor and Grant are
all in line acknowledging in patriotic salute the
eloquent words with which he has pictured them
on the records of our history.

Following them comes that great company of
statesmen whose voices were heard with his own
in the State House and Faneuil Hall at Boston,
or in the House or Senate Chamber at Washington: Webster, Calhoun and Clay, Adams and
Everett, John Bell, John P. Kennedy, Nathan
Appleton and William C. Rives, Thomas Benton
and Lewis Cass, Josiah Quincy and John H. Clifford, Robert J. Breckenridge and John J. Critten-
den; and among all those voices, now stilled
forever, where was one which spoke more often,
more feelingly for our Union and our Constitution
than Robert C. Winthrop?

The somewhat saddened procession of patriots,
remembered as more or less connected with our
country's storms and tempests, gives way to
another filled with the perpetual sunshine of

letters and the arts. The great singers go
marching by, headed by Dana, Halleck, Long-
fellow and Bryant.

In the broader field of literature the double
column widens into a battalion and brings us
numbers from beyond the seas, headed by Irving,
Motley, Prescott, Palfrey, Savage, Sparks and
Channing.

The true and only way to understand and
appreciate Mr. Winthrop's work is to read his
published addresses. They are an autobiography
of his own life and mind and a history of his
country and times, as well as a tribute to the
hundreds of great men with whom he has lived
and labored. His style is so simple and pure and
runs so smoothly that one can read his speeches
through consecutively without weariness. When
reading the orations of his great predecessor,
Webster, you feel as if you were always on
mountain tops, but reading Mr. Winthrop is like
a journey through his own beautiful New England, mounting at times to the highest altitudes
of thought and expression, but constantly dipping
into different grades—enjoying sometimes the
running stream, the babbling brook, the hum of
neighboring industry and the perfume of rural
flowers.

His eulogies of individuals have been truly
historical, and the salient points of their lives
have been skillfully formulated and presented.
Among his contemporaries might especially be
mentioned his eulogies upon Nathan Appleton,
Thomas Aspinwall, William H. Prescott, Josiah

Quincy, Edward Everett, John H. Clifford and George Peabody.

The various powers of the orator are admirably displayed by his beautiful treatment of those most capable men, all so great in character and works, yet so different and distinct in individual peculiarities.

But of all others his tributes to Washington, to Franklin, to Henry Clay, and Daniel Webster are preëminent. Did time permit I would select from his countless treasures a few jewels from each, and weave a chain of gems that you could carry away with you instead of any thoughts or words of my own, but time compels me to limit myself to a few specimens of his tributes to one subject only for illustration of his style and manner:

As long ago as 1837, while Mr. Webster was still alive, Mr. Winthrop said (Vol. I p. 216):—"The career of Mr. Webster is before the country. Let him retire when he will—he needs no defense, he requires no eulogy, he fears no investigation. Retire when he will, he will leave light, imperishable, unfading light behind him, and that not only gilding his own memory and casting glory upon our common wealth, but cheering and guiding and illuminating the path of constitutional patriotism throughout all generations. Other stars may have reached a higher ascension, may have sparkled with a more dazzling luster, may have shot with a wilder fire. Meteors too may have flashed and flamed and glared and cast a moment's wonder or a moment's fear and passed away. But as long as our glorious Constitution shall be borne up upon the waves of trial, and its banner of union and liberty be seen streaming to the winds, in every moment of doubt and danger the passengers and the pilot will be found

turning alike for their direction to our own Northern
Star,

> "Of whose true fixed and resting quality
> There is no fellow in the firmament."

In 1876 at the unvailing of Webster's statue in
Central Park, N. Y., he said (Vol. III. p. 438): "To
have seen and heard him on one of his field days was a
privilege, which no one will undervalue whoever enjoyed
it.   There was a power, a breadth, a beauty, a perfection
in some of his efforts which distanced all approach and
rendered rivalry ridiculous."

"Among those who have been celebrated as orators
or public speakers, in our own days or in other days,
there have been many diversities of gifts and many
diversities of operations.   There have been those who
were listened to wholly for their intellectual qualities,
for the wit or the wisdom, the learning or the philosophy,
which characterized their efforts.   There have been
those whose main attraction was a curious felicity and
facility of illustration and description, adorned by the
richest gems which could be gathered by historical re-
search or classical study.   There have been those to
whom the charms of manner and the graces of elocution
and the melody of voice were the all-sufficient recom-
mendations to attention and applause.   And there have
been those who owed their success more to opportunity
and occasion, to some stirring theme or some exciting
emergency, than to any peculiar attributes of their own.
But Webster combined everything.   No thoughts more
profound and weighty.   No style more terse and telling·
No illustrations more vivid and clear-cut.   No occasions
more august and momentous.   No voice more deep and
thrilling.   No manner more impressive and admirable.
No presence so grand and majestic, as his.

That great brain of his, as I have seen it working,
whether in public debate or in private converse, seemed
to me often like some mighty machine,—always ready
for action, and almost always in action, evolving
much material from its own resources and researches,

and eagerly appropriating and assimilating whatever was brought witin its reach, producing and reproducing the richest fabrics with the ease and certainty, the precision and the condensing energy, of a perfect Corliss engine.

And he put his own crown-stamp on almost every thing he uttered. There was no mistaking one of Webster's great efforts. There is no mistaking them now. They will be distinguished, in all time to come, like pieces of old gold or silver plate, by an unmistakable mint-mark. He knew, like the casters or forgers of yonder statue, not only how to pour forth burning words and blazing thoughts, but so to blend and fuse and weld together his facts and figures, his illustrations and arguments, his metaphors and subject matter, as to bring them all out at last into one massive and enduring image of his own great mind!"

When the Webster Centennial Banquet was held at Boston, January 18, 1882, it was thought that Mr. Winthrop would not be able to speak, or would feel as if he had already said all he could say. Our associate Mr. Dexter told me at the time, that he went on purpose to hear Mr. Winthrop and that it was one of the greatest treats of his life, and with one quotation from that evening's speech I will close:

(Vol. IV., p. 377.) "Living and dead he has been the theme of the most eloquent orators, of the most faithful and loving biographers of our land — Everett, and Choate, and Hillard, President Felton of Harvard, President Woods of Bowdoin, and Mr. Wm. M. Evarts—to name no others—have found in him the inspiration of some of their most celebrated efforts, who may well be content to live on the applauses and praises which their efforts have called forth from immediate hearers and admirers. They will enjoy at least a reflected and traditional fame. But Webster will always stand safest and strongest on his own showing. His fame will be independent of praise or dispraise from other men's lips. He can be measured to his full altitude, as a thinker, a writer, a speaker, only by the standard of his own im-

mortal productions. That masterly style, that pure
Saxon English, that clear and cogent statement, that
close and clinching logic, that power of going down to
the depths and up to the heights of any great argument,
letting the immaterial or incidental look out for itself,
those vivid descriptions, those magnificent metaphors,
those thrilling appeals,—not introduced as mere orna-
ments wrought out in advance and stored up for an
opportunity of display, but sparkling and blazing out in
the very heat of an effort, like gems uncovering themselves in the working of a mine,—these are some of the
characteristics which will secure for Webster a fame
altogether his own, and will make his works a model
and a study long after most of those who have praised
him, or who have censured him, shall be forgotten.

What if those six noble volumes of his were obliter-
ated from the roll of American literature and American
eloquence! What if those consummate defences of the
Constitution and the Union had never been uttered, and
their instruction and inspiration had been lost to us
during the fearful ordeal to which that Constitution and
that Union have since been subjected! Are we quite
sure that we should have had the Constitution, as it was,
and the Union as it is, to be fought for, if the birth we
are commemorating had never occurred,—if that bright
Northern Star had never gleamed above the hills of
New Hemisphere? Let it be, if you please, that its light
was not always serene and steady. Let it be that mist
and clouds sometimes gathered over its disk, and hid its
guiding rays from many a wistful eye. Say even, if
you will, that to some eyes it seemed once to be shoot-
ing madly from its sphere. Make every deduction
which his bitterest enemies have ever made for any
alleged deviation from the course which had been
marked out for it by others, or which it seemed to have
marked out for itself, in its path across the sky. Still,
still, there is radiance and glory enough left, as we contemplate its whole golden track, to make us feel and
acknowledge that it had no fellow in our firmament.

It may be truly said of Mr. Winthrop as
he said of Mr. Webster at the Webster centennial banquet in Boston in 1882 :

"After all, what are all the fine things which
have ever been said of him, or which ever can be
said of him, to-night or a hundred years hence,
compared with the splendid record which he has
left of himself as a debater in Congress and as an
orator before the people?   We do not search out
for what was *said* about Pericles or Demosthenes
or Cicero or Burke.   It is enough for us to read
their orations."

Mr. Winthrop will be remembered by different men in various characters as an historian, a
scholar, a statesman, a dispenser of hospitality to
distinguished visitors from the Old World, as a
Christian or a philanthropist.

But where and how will he be remembered
longest and best?

When the young men of future generations
pay their first visit to Bunker Hill, and behold
the speaking statue of Colonel Prescott, they will
surely be told to read of its graphic story from
the orator who unveiled it to an admiring popu-
lace.

When they behold the lifelike statue of the
philosopher and patriot Benjamin Franklin, in
front of the old court house in Boston, so near
the place of his birth and the grave of his
parents, they will be told by whom that statue
was inaugurated and the admirable oration pronounced upon its completion.

When they visit the memorials of our great

men in New York, and behold the colossal statue
of that colossal genius Daniel Webster, they will
be directed to the grand oration spoken at its first
exhibition by his pupil and friend, who more than
any other orator of our times has pictured him to
us in words that will live. When they visit the
sandy plains of Yorktown, one of their chief
delights will be the story there told before the
representatives of three nations upon the
hundredth anniversary of the triumph of American arms. When they repair to the capital of
our country and stand beside the monument to
Washington, of all the figures which will come
trooping before their excited imaginations there
will be few indeed which will stand out more
vividly than that of the tall, slender, courteous
orator who was part of its corner stone and its
capstone; and in fancy they will still hear his
ringing tones as he said: "Build it to the skies,
you cannot outreach the loftiness of his principles! Found it upon the massive and eternal
rock, you cannot make it more enduring than his
fame! Construct it of the peerless Parian
marble, you cannot make it purer than his life!
Exhaust upon it the rules and principles of
ancient and of modern art, you cannot make it
more proportionate than his character!"

(NO 1800)

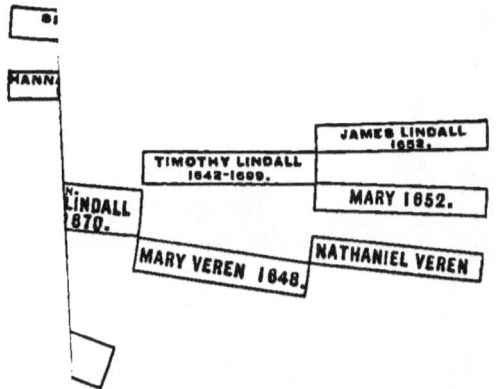

S.

HANNA

‍LINDALL
‍870.

TIMOTHY LINDALL
1642-1699.

JAMES LINDALL
1652.

MARY 1652.

MARY VEREN 1648.

NATHANIEL VEREN

APPENDIX.

RESOLUTIONS.

At the regular annual meeting of the Chicago Historical Society, on the 20th day of November, 1894, Mr. Edward G. Mason, President.

Upon motion of Mr. Daniel Goodwin, seconded by Mr. Charles Mulliken, the following memorial tribute was unanimously adopted.

WHEREAS, the Chicago Historical Society has learned through the Public Press of the death of the Hon. Robert C. Winthrop, who for many years has been one of our honorary members, and for fifty-five years was a distinguished member of the Massachusetts Historical Society, we desire to put upon our records our great estimate of the deceased as a historian, orator and philanthropist.

Mr. Winthrop came from historical stock, his father, Thomas Lyndall Winthrop having been for many years President of the Massachusetts Historical Society.

In his varied positions as member of the Massachusetts Legislature; of the House of Representatives and Senate of the United States; as President of the Massachusetts Historical Society for thirty years from 1855 to 1885; as President of the Bunker Hill Monument Association and as President of the Trustees of the Peabody Education Fund he has commemorated the lives of more than one hundred and fifty of the leading men of our own country and many of his great contemporaries of foreign lands, and has so accomplished the difficult tasks as to write a history not only of his own times but of our entire country from its cradle days until now. His eloquent pictures of the great men of this country will live for lovers of biography and history as long as we possess a national flag and an undivided country.

Like his predecessors in the United States Senate,

Daniel Webster and Edward Everett, his whole heart and his wonderful eloquence were devoted to the constitution of his country.

Plymouth chose him for the orator of the day on celebrating the 250th anniversary of the Landing of the Pilgrims on Plymouth Rock, December 21, 1870.

The City of Boston claimed him for her 100th anniversary on the 4th of July, 1876.

The City of New York chose him for her orator when the bronze statue of Daniel Webster was unvailed in Central Park in 1876.

The Bunker Hill Association selected him for its orator June 17, 1881, when Col. Prescott retook the hill where he led the most thrilling and picturesque battle since Marathon and Thermopylae.

The United States pointed to him as the foremost man of her then forty millions to deliver the oration at Yorktown on the 19th of October, 1881, the 100th anniversary of the final triumph of the patriot army.

He was the chosen orator of our Government to lay the corner stone of the Washington Monument at our National Capital in 1848, and to deliver the oration at its final completion in 1885

In these most conspicuous and trying positions Mr. Winthrop so acquitted himself as to answer the demands of the literary critic, the precise historian and the full-hearted patriot.

We cannot limit our eulogy to Mr. Winthrop as an historian and orator, for he was no less conspicuous as a Christian philantropist. As President of the Boston Provident Association for twenty-five years, he exhibited such skill in organization and administration as to point him out as the proper executive head of the great Charitable Trust endowed by George Peabody in 1867, and which in the extent and magnitude of its charities and the exalted station of its directors eclipses everything of its kind in history. Therefore, be it

Resolved, that a copy of this memorial minute be spread upon our records, and that copies of the same be sent to Massachusetts Historical Society, to the Trustees of the Peabody Education Fund, and to the American Historical Society.

LIST OF MR. WINTHROP'S EULOGIES.

	TIME	DELIVERED	VOL.	PAGE
Adams, John........	1735-1826	Dec. 16, 1873	3	293
Adams, John Q......	1767-1848	Feb. 24, 1848	1	614
Agassiz, Louis.......	1807-1873	April 16,1874	3	312
Aiken, Gov. Wm	1806			---
Ames, Seth..........	1805-1881	Sept. 8, 1881	4	280
Appleton, Nathan....	1779-1861	Aug. 8, 1861	2	502
Appleton, Samuel ...	1766-1853	Sept. 17, 1855	2	222
Appleton, William ...	1786-1862	Feb. 18, 1862	--	516
Aspinwall, Col. Thos.	1786-1876	Oct. 12, 1876	3	432
Bacon, Rev. Leonard.	1802-1881	July 12, 1882	4	372
Barnes, Gen. Jos. K ..	1817-1883	Oct. 3, 1883	4	452
Bartlett, Wm. S.......	1809-1883	Dec. 13, 1883	4	474
Bell, Luther V.......	1806-1862	Mar. 13, 1862	2	515
Bigelow, Dr. Jacob...	1787-1879	Feb. 13, 1879	4	23
Bigelow, ErastusB ...	1814-1879	Dec. 11, 1879	4	111
Bowdoin James	1727-1790	Sept. 5, 1849	1	90
Bowdoin, James......	1752-1811	Sept. 5, 1849	1	90
Brooks, William G...	1807-1879	Jan. 9, 1879	4	18
Bryant, William C .	1794-1878	June 13, 1878	3	510
Budington, William I.	1815-1879	Dec. 11, 1879	4	114
Bulloch, Alexander H.	1816-1882	Feb. 9, 1882	4	381
Burton, John Hill	1809-1881	Sept. 8, 1881	4	281
Calhoun, John C	1782-1850	April 1, 1850	1	651
Chadbourne, Paul A .	1824-1883	Mar. 8, 1883	4	4:1
Channing, Wm. E ...	1780-1842	April 18,1880	4	131
Chastellux, Mqs. de ..	1734-1788	May 13, 1859	2	485
Circourt, Adolph de..	1800-1879	Jan. 8, 1880	4	116
Clay, Henry	1777-1852	Aug. 1879	4	39
Clifford, Gov. John H.	1809-1876	Jan. 13, 1876	3	342
Crittenden, J. J	1787-1863	Aug. 13, 1863	2	558
Cushing, Caleb	1800-1879	Jan. 9, 1879	4	19
Dana, Richard II	1815-1882	Jan. 12, 1882	4	372
Dante	1265-1321	May 11, 1865	2	664
Davis, George T	1810-1877	Oct. 11, 1877	3	477
Davis, Gov. John	1787-1854	April 26,1854	2	179
Dearborn, Henry	1751-1829	April 10,1884	4	319 495
Dearborn, Henry A.S.	1783-1851	April 10, 1884	4	496
Dexter, George	-1883	Jan. 10, 1884	4	481
Dix, John A	1798-1879	May 8, 1879	4	34
Emerson, Geo. B....	1797-1881	Mar. 10, 1881	4	229
Everett, Edward	1794-1865	Jan. 30, 1865	2	653
Felton, Cornelius C..	1807-1862	Mar. 13, 1862	2	517

	TIME	DELIVERED	VOL.	PAGE
Fillmore, Millard ___	1800–1874	Mar. 12, 1874	3	307
Folsom, Chas _____	1794–1872	Dec. 12, 1872	3	186
Frothingham, Nath'l.	1793–1870	April 14,1870	3	66
Frothingham, Richr'd	1812–1880	Feb. 12, 1880	4	125
Goddard, Delano A __	–1882	July 12, 1882	4	373
Graham, William A__	1801–1875	Oct. 6, 1875	3	326
Grant, Gen. U. S_ ___	1822–1885	Oct. 7, 1885	4	574
Gray, John C ___ ___	1793–1881	Mar. 10, 1881	4	227
Grigsby, Hugh Blair_	1806–1881	May 12, 1881	4	235
Grinnell, Joseph ___	1789–1885	Jan. 13, 1876	3	344
Hancock, John_____	1737–1793	Sept. 17, 1856	2	273
Haven, Samuel F ___	1806–1881	Sept. 8, 1881	4	281
Hillard, Geo. S _____	1808–1879	Feb. 13, 1879	4	26
Hudson, Chas ____	1795–1881	May 12, 1881	4	233
Jones, John Winter __	1791–1881	Sept. 8, 1881	4	281
Kennedy, John P ___	1795–1870	Sept. 8, 1870	3	69
King, Daniel P _____	1801–1850	July 27, 1850	1	697
King, Rufus _____	1755–1827	Nov. 20, 1854	2	200
Knox,Maj-Gen.Henry	1750–1806	May 27, 1857	2	348
Laboulaye, Edw. R. L.	1811–1883	June 14, 1883	4	425
Lafayette, Gen ___	1757–1834	Oct. 19, 1881	4	333
Langdon, Elwyn Alf'd	1804–1883	April 10,1884	4	494
Lawrence, Abbott____	1792–1855	Aug. 20, 1855	2	210
Lenox, James_____	1800–1880	Mar. 11, 1880	4	128
Lincoln, Abraham _	1809–1865	April 29,1865	2	661
Livermore, Geo ___	§1809–1865	Sept. 14, 1865	2	667
Lowell, John A _____	1797–1881	Nov. 10, 1881	4	364
Luther, Martin _____	1483–1546	Nov. 10, 1883	4	467
Lyman, Theodore ___	1792–1849	Oct. 24, 1885	4	608
Lyndhurst, Lord_____	1772–1863	Nov. 12, 1863	2	567
Manning, Thomas C__	–1887	Oct. 3, 1888		
Martin, M. Henri ____	1810–1883	Jan. 10, 1884	4	479
McIlvaine, Bishop ___	1799–1873	July 16, 1873	3	255
Mendelssohn _____	1809–1847	May 21, 1857	2	341
Metcalf, Theron _____	1784–1875	Dec. 9, 1875	3	341
Mignet, Francis A ___	1796–1884	April 10,1884	4	487
Miles, James B_____	1822–1875	Dec. 9, 1875	3	340
Minot, William _____	1783–1874	Mar. 12, 1874	3	302
Motley, John Lothrop	1814–1877	June 14, 1877	3	467
Newell, William _____	1803–1881	Nov. 10, 1881	4	364
Palfrey, Dr. John G__	1796–1881	May 12, 1881	4	238
Parker, Francis E ____		Feb. 11, 1886	4	586
Peabody, George ____	1795–1869	Feb. 8, 1870	3	36
Perkins, Thomas H __	1764–1854	Oct. 1854	4	575
Phillips, John C_____	1839–1885	Mar. 12, 1885	4	555
Preble, Geo. H_____	1816–1885	Mar. 12, 1885	4	555
Prescott, Col. William	1726–1795	June 17, 1881	4	253
Prescott, William H__	1796–1859	Feb. 1, 1859	2	405
Quincy, Edmund ____	1808–1877	June 14, 1877	3	465

	TIME	DELIVERED	VOL.	PAGE
Quincy, Eliza S..........	1798–1884	Feb. 14, 1884	4	485
Quincy, Josiah........	1744–1775	Dec. 21, 1853	2	140
Quincy, Josiah, Jr .	1772–1864	July 14, 1864	2	584
Sears, David..........	1787–1871	Feb. 2, 1881	3	138
Sears, Barnas.........	1802–1880	Feb. 2, 1881	4	206
Sparks, Jared	1789–1866	April 3, 1866	2	670
Salisbury, Stephen....	1798–1884	Oct. 9, 1884	4	515
Seward, William H ..	1800–1872	Dec. 12, 1872	3	190
Somerby, Horatio G .	1805–1872	Dec. 12, 1872	3	187
Stanhope, Earl....	1805–1875	Jan. 13, 1876	3	357
Stanley, Dean A. P ..	1815–1881	Sept. 8, 1881	4	283
Sumner, Chas	1811–1874	Mar. 12, 1874	3	309
Taney, Roger B	1777–1864	Mar. 13, 1873	3	245
Taylor, Zachary	1784–1850	June 26, 1872	3	173
Taylor, Richard	1826–1879	Oct. 1, 1879	4	90
Thayer, Nathaniel ...	1808–1883	Mar. 8, 1883	4	412
Thomas, Benj. F	1813–1878	Oct. 10, 1878	3	524
Ticknor, George......	1791–1871	Feb. 9, 1871	3	140
Tuttle, Chas. Wesley.	1829–1881	Sept. 8, 1881	4	279
Upham, Charles W ..	1802–1875	Oct. 14, 1875	3	331
Verplanck, Gulian C .	1796–1870	April 14, 1870	3	64
Visconti, Baron L. T. J	1791–1853	Jan. 24, 1881	4	199
Waite, Morrison R...	1816–1888	Oct. 3, 1888		
Walker, Pres. James .	1794–1874	Oct. 14, 1875	3	330
" " " ..	" "	Feb. 18, 1878	3	500
Warren, Judge Chas.H	....	Oct. 14, 1875	3	330
Washburne, Emory...	1799–1877	April 11, 1877	3	457
Washington, Geo	1732–1799	July 4, 1848	1	70
" "	" "	May 27, 1857	2	346
" " ...	" "	June 17, 1857	2	351
" "	" "	Feb. 22, 1863	2	553
" "	" . "	Feb. 22, 1873	3	236
" "	" "	Feb. 22, 1885	4	525
Watson, Samuel	–1877	Oct. 3, 1877	3	475
Webster, Daniel	1782–1852	Feb. 15, 1837	1	216
" " ....·	" "	May 21, 1857	2	335
" "	" "	Nov. 25, 1876	3	436
" " ...	" "	Jan. 18, 1882	4	375
Wetmore, Samuel....	1812–1885	Oct. 7, 1885	4	573
Wilson, Henry.......	1812–1875	Dec. 9, 1875	3	340
*Winthrop, Benj. R...	1804–1879	Sept. 11, 1879	4	85
Woods, Leonard	1707–1807	Jan. 9, 1879	4	22
Wyman, Jeffries	1814–1874	Feb. 18, 1878	3	502

*Gov. John, Life and Letters, 1864-1867, 2 vols.

This list ends in 1886. Later Eulogies are scattered through the published proceedings of the different societies of which Mr. Winthrop was a member.

MR. WINTHROP'S ESTIMATE OF ABRAHAM LINCOLN.

(Vol. II. 661.)

Beyond all doubt the life of President Lincoln was a thousand fold the most precious life in our whole land; and there are few of us I think who would not willingly have rescued it at the risk, or even at the sacrifice of our own. The cheerful courage, the shrewd sagacity—the earnest zeal, the imperturbable good nature, the untiring fidelity to duty, the ardent devotion to the Union, the firm reliance upon God, which he has displayed during his whole administration; and the eminent moderation and magnanimity, both toward political opponents and public enemies, which he has manifested since his recent and triumphant reëlection, have won for him a measure of regard and of respect and of affection such as no other man of our age has ever enjoyed.

IN RE THE DEARBORNS.

BOSTON, 2 April, 1884.

Dear Mr. Goodwin:—I thank you sincerely for the copy of your "Dearborns," which you have kindly sent me, and still more for the discourse itself. I have read it with great interest and gratification, and I cordially congratulate you on so successful a production. If you could send me another copy, addressed on the cover or fly leaf to the Massachusetts Historical Society from yourself, I should take pleasure in presenting it publicly at their annual meeting on the 10th inst. A copy should go to the library of Bowdoin College. I rejoice that the names of these good old friends of my boyhood and early manhood are so pleasantly and deservedly reviewed.

Yours truly,

ROBT. C. WINTHROP.

In presenting the book to the Massachusetts Historical Society, Mr. Winthrop said (Vol. IV., page 595), I must not conclude these introductory remarks without presenting to our library, in the name of Daniel Goodwin Esq., of Chicago, a very interesting and notable memoir of "The Dearborns,"—a commemorative discourse delivered before the Chicago Historical Society, on the eightieth anniversary of the occupation of Fort Dearborn and the first settlement of Chicago, in December last. It gives an excellent account of the career and character of General Henry Dearborn, and of his son General Henry Alexander Scammell Dearborn, both of whom were long conspicuous in the history of our country and our commonwealth; and it is illustrated by portraits of them both. The father was a gallant officer of the Revolution from Bunker Hill to Yorktown, and afterwards Secretary of War and Commander-in-Chief of the United States Army. The son was Collector of the Customs in this city, a member of Congress from Norfolk, first President of the Massachusetts Horticultural Society, and prominently associated with the erection of the Bunker Hill Monument and the establishment of the Mount Auburn cemetery.

Our thanks are due and will be returned, with the sanction of the Society to Mr. Goodwin, for so just and admirable a tribute to these patriotic and public-spirited men, so long known and honored in our community.

IN RE EDWIN C. LARNED.

Those who have read Mr. Larned's great argument in the Fugitive Slave case will be interested to read Mr. Winthrop's speeches in favor of a jury trial, and the right of the slave to the writ of habeas corpus and against the extension of slavery, or slave territory, and in favor of the admission of California under a constitution prohibiting slavery. The world is accustomed to think of Mr. Winthrop as a conservative and of Mr. Larned as radical, but the sentiments, and principles, and moral convictions of the two were identical. The two following letters will explain themselves:

BOSTON, 20 April, 1886.

Dear Mr. Goodwin:—Your handsome volume, in memory of Edwin C. Larned, came this morning.

I desire to acknowledge it gratefully without delay. I am just breaking up my winter home with a view to returning to Brookline after a journey of three or four weeks. I must therefore postpone doing justice to your memoir until I am established in summer quarters. I have read enough of it, however, to feel sure that I shall be interested in reading the whole.

Believe me, with kind regards

Yours truly,

ROBT. C. WINTHROP.

BROOKLINE, MASS., 6 July, 1886.

Dear Mr. Goodwin:—I have at last found an hour in my summer retirement to read the book you kindly sent me many weeks ago, "In Memory of Edwin C. Larned." I can now thank you for it intelligently. Your address is admirable, and so is that of Bishop Harris; the whole volume illustrates a character of great energy. The argument in the Fugitive Slave rescue is strong and brilliant, and exhibits power and eloquence. I had never known Mr. Larned and am not sure that I had ever heard of him until I read this volume. But I shall remember him henceforth as one whom it must have been a privilege to know, and whose memory it must be a pleasure to you to recall and illustrate. Accept my thanks for the volume and believe me.

Very truly yours,
Robt. C. Winthrop.

LETTERS.

The following letter was written by Mr. Winthrop after perusal of the foregoing essay prepared for the Chicago Literary Club.

BROOKLINE, 21 Nov., 1888.

Dear Mr. Goodwin:—You have been at great pains in describing my career and I thank you for all your kind and complimentary expressions. Your list of the persons I have noticed at greater or less length has come duly, and I return it with the addition of three names, Judge Manning of Louisiana, Chief Justice Waite of Ohio, and Gov. Wm. Aiken of South Carolina. These tributes are in our two last serials of the Peabody proceedings, published since my fourth volume was made up. The list is really a portentous one, reminding me forcibly of the great number of friends who have passed away since I began my public or quasi public life. All of them were associated with me either in Congress or in the Historical Society, or on the Peabody Board, and my notices of them have been in the way of duty.

You ask about my portraits. Eastman Johnson took a crayon of me when I was early in Congress, and when he was just beginning his career as an artist. Healy painted a kit-cat portrait of me in 1846; Huntington of New York painted a large family portrait of me in 1870. He also painted the full length of me in 1881-2, which is in the Speaker's corridor at Washington, presented by citizens of Massachusetts in recognition of my Yorktown oration. Huntington has since painted a third original of me for the Historical Society, of Massachusetts, on my withdrawal from thirty years presidency in 1885. There is a medallion of me by Ball Hughes in 1841 and a lithograph by a celebrated French artist taken in Paris, in 1847.

Accept my renewed acknowledgements of the trouble you have taken in reviewing my record and for the compliments you have paid me and believe me.

Very truly yours,

ROBT. C. WINTHROP.

BOSTON, March 21, 1889.

Dear Mr. Goodwin:—I thank you for sending me the little volume of sermons by our lamented friend Bishop Harris. Gov. Baldwin sent me a copy of his Bohlen lectures some years ago, and I have known him personally and have heard him preach at our Trinity Church. He was one of our ablest and best bishops, and he has been called higher too soon for every one but himself. I shall read these select sermons from time to time with great interest. Believe me, with kind regards to Mrs. Goodwin,   Yours very truly,

ROBT. C. WINTHROP.

P.S. I send you in a large envelope two of my latest productions: one a long notice of Washington, the other a shorter notice of John Winthrop. I prepared them at the request of the editors of Appleton's New Cyclopedia of American Biography—just published—the publishers sent me a few oversheets containing both articles, and I send you one of each.

BROOKLINE, MASS., May 22, 1890.

Dear Mr. Goodwin:—I returned home recently to find my table crowded with books, letters and pamphlets which had accumulated during a month's absence. I had been at New York, Washington and Richmond; and time had taken the opportunity to add another unit to the number of my years.

I avail myself of a moment's leisure to thank you for the kind expressions of your letter on my birthday.

I have entered my 82d in better condition than I had any right or reason to anticipate. But I am glad to be quietly established in my summer home, where I can "rest and be thankful." I was grieved to see the announcement of Wirt Dexter's death. He spent an an hour with me at Beverly farms last summer, while I was passing a few days with my son. I thought he was good for twenty years more of life and usefulness.

Believe me, with kind regards to your wife,

Yours very truly,

ROBT. C. WINTHROP.

MR. WINTHROP'S ADDRESS UPON THE FLAG
OF OUR UNION.

When I sent my essay to Mr. Winthrop in November, 1888, I asked him if there was any other point in his career in which he would rather be remembered than the memorable one alluded to in my peroration; with the exquisite courtsey which never failed him, and which Dr. Ellis says he never saw omitted in a friendly intercourse of more than half a century, Mr. Winthrop gave me to understand that my choice was unexception able, but still that his heart preferred one other and that was "my utterances on the 'Flag of the Union,' in concluding my speech on Boston common when presenting a United States flag to Col. Wilson's regiment on its departure for the war in October, 1861."

Let us learn then to recall and remember him as he himself would most love to be remembered and let his own eloquent words close this chapter of our lives.

The tall and graceful orator was standing on Boston common in sight and almost within hearing of the houses and streets where he and six generations of his patriot sires had lived since 1630—overhead were waving the old elms under which he and his ancestors had walked and played since before the Revolution —before him was a regiment of young men who had grown up in the streets of Boston within sight of the great monument, the old State House, the old South Church, all of them going out to meet death and many of them to fall and die and never more to return. They were led by Henry Wilson, who left the United States Senate for the battle field and who was afterward elected vice-president of the Union with the immortal Lincoln. Thus environed and thus placed as he should be sometime in enduring bronze, our great and departed orator spoke the words he would have his countrymen take home to their hearts.

"I have said enough and more than enough to manifest the spirit in which this flag is now committed to your charge. It is the National ensign, pure and simple; dearer to all our hearts at this moment as we lift it to the gale and see no other sign of hope upon the storm-cloud which rolls and rattles above it, save that which is reflected from its own radiant hues; dearer to us all than ever it was before, while gilded by the sunshine of prosperity and playing with the zephyrs of peace. It will speak for itself, far more eloquently than I can speak for it.

Behold it! listen to it! Every star has a tongue; every stripe is articulate. There is no language or speech where their voices are not heard. There's magic in the web of it. It has an answer for every question of duty. It has a solution for every doubt and every perplexity. It has a word of good cheer for every hour of gloom or of despondency.

Behold it! Listen to it! It speaks of earlier and of later struggles. It speaks of victories and sometimes of reverses, on the sea and on the land. It speaks of patriots and heroes among the living and among the dead and of him, the first and greatest of them all, around whose consecrated ashes this unnatural and abhorrent strife has so long been raging. But before all and above all other associations and memories — whether of glorious men, of glorious deeds, or glorious places—its voice is ever of Union and Liberty, of the constitution and the laws.

Behold it! Listen to it. Let it tell the story of its birth to these gallant volunteers as they march beneath its folds by day or repose beneath its sentinel stars by night. Let it recall to them the strange eventful history of its rise and progress; let it rehearse to them the wondrous tale of its trials and its triumphs, in peace as well as in war; and whatever

else may happen to it or to them it will never be surrendered to rebels; never be ignominiously struck to
treason; nor ever be prostituted to any unworthy
and un-Christian purpose of revenge, depredation or
rapine. And may a merciful God cover the head of
each one of its brave defenders in the hour of battle."